Do you know where

Sea Turtles

go?

Written by
Paul Lowery

Illustrated by
Tim Thomas

Do you know where Sea Turtles go?

It is the objective of the author and illustrator of this book, to provide sufficient information in a fun and informative way, for children to learn the importance of protecting the sea turtles and therefore produce a positive influence on our environment.

Paul Lowery

Paul Lowery *

Do you know where Sea Turtles go?

ISBN 0-9792379-0-4
ISBN 978-0-9792379-0-4
First Edition Revised 2007

Copyright 2005
by PBL Stories Inc
Panama City, FL 32444

Author: Paul Lowery
Illustrator: Tim Thomas

*For additional information please contact the publisher at:
PBL STORIES, LLC
2310 S. Hwy 77
Suite 110 PMB 393
Lynn Haven, FL 32444
www.pblstories.com • booksales@pblstores.com

First Edition
Published by: Thomas Expressions Inc.

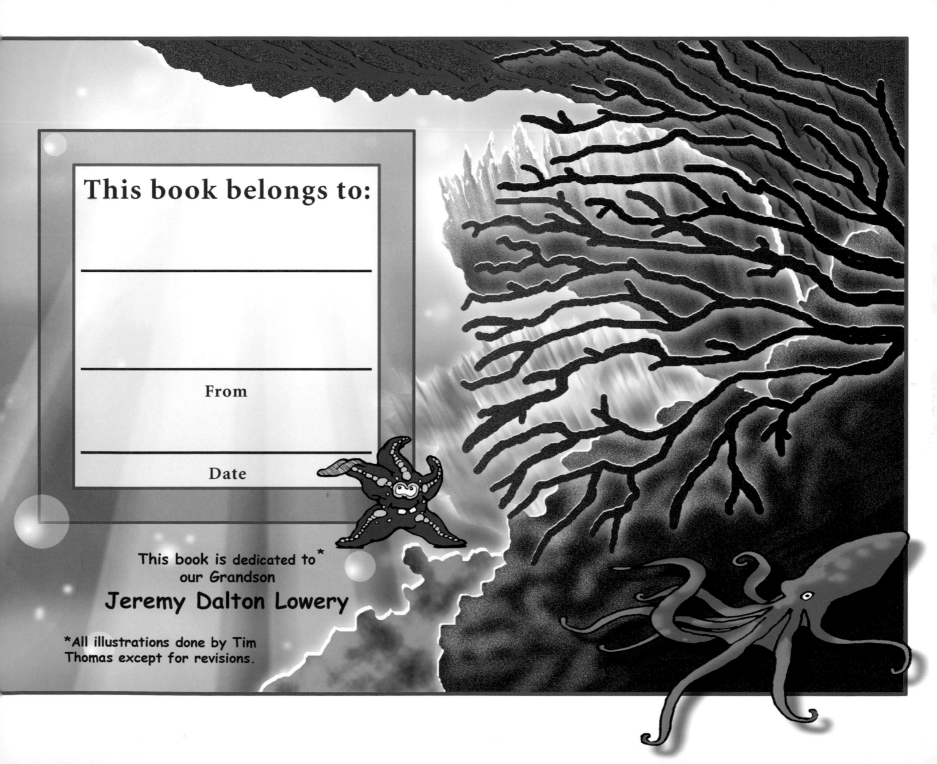

This book belongs to:

_____

_____

From

_____

Date

This book is dedicated to*
our Grandson
Jeremy Dalton Lowery

*All illustrations done by Tim
Thomas except for revisions.

My name is Myrtle and I'm a Sea Turtle,
a Loggerhead to be more precise.

I was hatched on the land, from under the sand,
where it is cozy, warm and nice.

**Mother dug a deep hole so we couldn't be found
and we hatched from our eggs, deep in the ground.**

Our eggs were covered with love, until we would hatch.
I had many brothers and sisters, in fact a whole batch.

I climbed up through the sand until I was at the top.
I was off on a race and I just couldn't stop.

There were many enemies just waiting to eat,
little sea turtles that are slow on their feet.

But I was too fast, I knew how to flee,
I made tracks on the beach as I ran toward the sea.

I dodged crabs in my path as sea gulls screamed past.
They couldn't catch me, because I was too fast.

As I entered the water, a new journey began,
that would last all my lifetime of oceans and sand.

I found a bed of seaweed that floated with the tide.
I climbed on to eat breakfast and enjoyed a free ride.

I began to grow bigger, and I felt a strong need,
to swim free in the ocean and leave my bed of seaweed.

I looked all around, and found I was alone.
The current swept me away, to places unknown.

I found I could hold my breath for an hour under the sea.
It was a special time of discovery filled with challenges for me.

There were all kinds of places I came to know,
in a lifetime of travel, in my new world below.

**There were dolphins and starfish and seahorses and snails
and sharks and octopuses and tuna and whales.**

I swam by beautiful coral reefs and tropical isles.
I was never in a hurry, but swam thousand of miles.

No matter where I went or how far I did roam.
I was never afraid because I was always at home.

My home was my shell colored yellow and green,
that protected me from all kinds of sea creatures that were mean.

My life was very happy as I swam on my way,
so it was that I met a new friend to play with one day.

He was a very handsome turtle and there was romance in the air.
The coral reefs were beautiful and we made a very lovely pair.

We played together each day and rested each night,
in a sea turtle paradise, what a beautiful sight.

But, one day we parted, I had a current to catch.
I traveled many miles back, so my babies could hatch.

I swam back to the beach where my journey had begun,
and laid all of my eggs, just as my mother had done.

I covered them with love and crawled back to the sea,
and asked God in a prayer, for their protection and safety.

Loggerhead

Hawksbill

Kemp's Ridley

Green Sea Turtle

Sea turtles are endangered and we need to make sure,
that they all are protected, that they can endure.

Leatherback

There are Loggerheads and Leatherbacks that nest on our shores,
some Hawksbills, the Green Turtle and maybe some more.

The next time you see one, don't harm it in any way.
Who knows what places it will swim to one day?

**So if you want to find out where sea turtles go,
just adopt one from the next page, track it, and you will know.***

St. Andrews State Park

PANAMA CITY BEACH, FL

Well known for its sugar white sands and emerald green waters, this former military reservation has over one-and-a-half miles of beaches on the Gulf of Mexico and Grand Lagoon.

St. Andrews State Park has been protecting sea turtles and monitoring their nesting activity for over 30 years. During the 5 month nesting season (May through September) Sea turtle nests within the State Park are marked, observed and evaluated daily to collect data that will aid scientist in their efforts to assure the greatest opportunity for turtle nesting success.

Rick Wiles
Park Service Specialist
St. Andrews State Park
Panama City Beach, Florida USA

The Florida-based Caribbean Conservation Corporation (CCC) designed and sponsored the establishment of the sea turtle license plate in 1997 by presenting state lawmakers with over 10,000 petitions and a marketing plan for the new tag. The turtle tag quickly became one of the most popular specialty plates in Florida, raising over $1 million annually. The turtle plate is also one of the least expensive specialty plates in Florida.

"Over 90% of all the sea turtle nesting in the United States takes place in Florida," said CCC Executive Director David Godfrey.

"We established the tag to provide a permanent funding source for turtle research and protection programs being conducted by State biologists and the many independent turtle protection groups working in Florida."

Caribbean Conservation Corporation
4424 NW 13th St. Suite #A1
Gainesville, FL 32609
1-800-678-7853
ccc@cccturtle.org

All of the funding generated by the tag is required by law to support sea turtle protection in Florida.

Adopt-A-Turtle!
For more information call
1-800-678-7853 or www.cccturtle.org